Ziggy and the
the
#3

Black Dinosaurs

Shadows of Caesar's Creek

By Sharon M. Draper
Illustrated by Jesse Joshua Watson

Aladdin Paperbacks
New York London Toronto Sydney

This book is dedicated to Jasmine and Landon

☙

ALADDIN PAPERBACKS
An imprint of Simon & Schuster Children's Publishing Division
1230 Avenue of the Americas, New York, NY 10020
Text copyright © 1997, 2006 by Sharon M. Draper
Illustrations copyright © 2006 by Jesse Joshua Watson
All rights reserved, including the right of reproduction
in whole or in part in any form.
ALADDIN PAPERBACKS and colophon are trademarks of
Simon & Schuster, Inc.
Designed by Lisa Vega
The text of this book was set in Minion.
Manufactured in the United States of America
First Aladdin Paperbacks edition June 2006
4   6   8   10   9   7   5   3
Library of Congress Control Number 2005930999
ISBN-13: 978-0-689-87913-5
ISBN-10: 0-689-87913-X

Shadows of Caesar's Creek

One

Ziggy's thoughts bounced like hot popcorn as he ran through his backyard to the clubhouse of the Black Dinosaurs. *An overnight camping trip!* he thought eagerly. *Fishing! Hiking! Cooking over a campfire!* He couldn't wait to talk to Rico, Rashawn, and Jerome, the other members of the Black Dinosaurs, about the letter from Camp Caesar.

Ziggy's huge backyard was wonderful. It was a place where flowers, weeds, rabbits, and ten-year-old boys could grow wild. It was a place to dream and create—a perfect location for secrets and adventures. Ziggy followed a path, probably used by raccoons, which ran back through the thick under-brush to the clubhouse.

Using the remains of an old fence that the boys had found in Ziggy's backyard, they had built the clubhouse themselves the previous summer. They had cut holes that looked a lot like windows in the two side walls, and for the door, they'd used a smaller section of the fence wall. It closed with a bent piece of wire coat hanger.

Inside, the clubhouse was about ten feet by twelve feet—not really big, but large enough for four boys to sit and talk. In it was one lawn chair with most of the webbing missing, one folding chair left over from a church picnic, one three-legged kitchen chair (they used a large rock to balance it), and a bicycle with two flat tires. This was their seating arrange-ment, or they could push everything aside and sit on the blanket that Ziggy's mom had given them.

Just as Ziggy got to the front of the clubhouse, he tripped over his shoelace, lost his balance, landed on his backside, and rolled with a laugh to the door, where Jerome was waiting for him. Ziggy never walked anywhere—he bounced or jogged or galloped wherever he went. He was always in a good mood, always excited about whatever was happening around him. So Jerome was not surprised when Ziggy landed at his feet, bubbling with excitement.

He helped Ziggy up and asked with a laugh, "What's up, Ziggy?"

"Did your letter come, mon? Are you packed? Where are Rico and Rashawn?" Ziggy's eyes were bright. Behind him, the boys could hear the rustling of something in the bushes.

Rashawn's Siberian husky, Afrika, with one blue eye and one brown eye, trotted out of the bushes, found his favorite spot under a tree, and went to sleep. Rashawn, tall, brown, and skinny, and wearing his favorite army boots, stomped through the backyard and sat down on a large rock in front of the clubhouse.

"What's goin' on, fellas?" he asked. "Where's Rico?"

Ziggy was still hopping around enthusiastically. He wore a green vest, a blue shirt, and bright red jeans. Today a large knitted cap covered his braids, which usually bounced as much as he did. Ziggy's family had come from Jamaica to Ohio several years before and had moved onto the street in Cincinnati where Rico, Rashawn, and Jerome lived. The four boys had been friends since first grade.

Rico was coming down the path to the clubhouse. He had a huge wad of bubble gum in his mouth and was attempting to blow the world's biggest bubble. He walked slowly, concentrating on blowing and balancing the bubble, which was almost the size of his face. He didn't see Ziggy, who leaped into the air, bursting to tell his good news.

"It's almost time!" cried Ziggy. As Ziggy began to speak, he waved his arms around wildly. At that moment Rico and his bubble walked right into Ziggy's hand. *Splat!* went the bubble gum, and Rico's surprised face and thick brown hair were instantly covered with sticky pink bubble gum.

Rashawn and Jerome hooted with laughter; Ziggy rolled on the ground with delight. Rico didn't laugh much. But it was clear he wasn't angry as he sat on the grass, picking gum out of his hair.

"That bubble would have gone in the *Guinness Book of World Records*," he said, faking disappointment. "I bet it was the biggest one in the world so far!"

"Aw, mon, I blow bubbles bigger than that every day!" boasted Ziggy. "But you gotta mix the bubble gum with mashed potatoes first! That's the secret ingredient!"

"Yuck!" exclaimed the others. They were used to Ziggy's unusual tastes in food. He stirred his chocolate milk with pickles and put mustard on his cornflakes.

"So tell us, Ziggy," Jerome said finally. "What's up?"

"The mailman just left," Ziggy told them, "and my letter from Camp Caesar came today! We've been waiting forever, but the trip is finally here! We're going camping at Caesar's Creek State Park next week!"

"We got our letters today too," Rico said. "It's gonna be a cool trip." He had almost finished pulling the bubble gum out of his hair.

Rashawn cheered. "Let's hear it for my dad!" Rashawn's father was a member of the Black Heritage Club. They had decided several months ago to sponsor field trips for the young people of the community, and this camping trip was one of the first activities.

"I've never slept outside in the woods before," admitted Jerome. "I wonder what we ought to take."

Ziggy pulled a folded piece of paper from the back pocket of his red jeans. "Not to worry, mon!" he announced. "Here's the list of things to bring. Let's see here . . . flashlight, sleeping bag, backpack, extra socks, bug spray . . ."

"Bug spray?" asked Jerome. He hated insects. He carried bug spray every day in his book bag, just in case. "You know how I am about bugs! I'll probably never get to sleep, looking for bugs in the night."

Ziggy laughed and said again, "Not to worry, mon! It will be so dark in those woods at night you'll never even *see* the bugs that bite you!"

Jerome picked up a handful of dry leaves and threw them at Ziggy. "Hey, you really know how to make a dude feel better, man!"

"Who else is going?" asked Rico.

"I'm not sure," Rashawn answered. "I think a few more kids from school. There might be some kids from other schools near the campsite, my dad said."

"Any girls?" asked Rashawn.

"Who cares, mon!" Ziggy replied. "I'm more concerned with the lions and tigers and bears!"

"There are no lions and tigers in the woods here in Ohio," Rico declared. "But I'm not sure about bears."

"Bears?" asked Rashawn fearfully.

"There's no bears around here," Jerome stated, "but I know the woods are full of bugs!"

"Don't forget, we'll have bug spray," reminded Rico.

"Bug spray won't do much against a bear!" muttered Rashawn, who didn't want to admit he was a little worried.

Ziggy checked the list again. "Not to worry,

mon," he announced again with cheerful assurance, "nothing on here about bears!"

"That doesn't mean there aren't any," Rashawn continued, smiling in spite of himself.

"What about Indians?" asked Rico.

"I don't know," Jerome said with a frown. "There used to be millions of Indians in Ohio—a long time ago."

"What do you suppose happened to all of them?" Rico wondered.

"Hey, mon, I bet there are thousands of Indians living in the woods up there right now!"

"No, Ziggy," Rico said thoughtfully, "I think they got pushed out—from their own land. My dad told me that it used to be really beautiful around here before there were roads or bridges or even houses."

"Can you imagine," Rashawn thought out loud, "nothing but forests for miles and miles? The Indians had it so good!"

"Yeah, except for one thing." Jerome grinned.

"What, mon?"

"There was no place to stop for hamburgers and French fries!"

"Or pizza!"

"Or tacos!"

"Or chocolate-covered spaghetti, mon!"

At that, they all grabbed dry leaves and grass from the yard to throw at Ziggy, until he ran laughing and shouting through the backyard.

"Not to worry, mon!" they heard him yell in the distance, still laughing. "I'll bring my own!"

TWO

The following Saturday dawned bright and clear. Jerome, wearing his uncle's tall black hiking boots and black leather vest, waited in the parking lot with his grandmother and his two little sisters, Temika and LaTonya. They were still sleepy and a little grumpy that they had been made to get up just so Jerome could go on a trip. But nobody argued with Granny. When she said get up, that's what you did.

Jerome's backpack and sleeping bag, which were a faded army green, had belonged to his grandfather, who had fought in the Vietnam War. Jerome wore dark sunglasses and tried not to look excited as the camp bus pulled into the lot.

Rico's mom drove a dull brown car that badly needed a muffler and a paint job. It rattled and sputtered and coughed into the parking lot, just behind the bus. Rico grinned at Jerome and hopped out almost before the car stopped. He was dressed in blue jeans and a matching blue shirt, which was, as usual, neatly tucked in. He even had a matching blue sleeping bag and backpack.

Jerome knew without looking that Rico's backpack would have neat rolls of clothes, with a toothbrush in a plastic holder and extra plastic bags for wet socks. The others sometimes teased Rico about his organization, but they knew they could depend on him to build anything they needed—from clubhouses to tree bridges.

The other kids who were going on the trip quickly began to fill the parking lot. Tiana was a tall, pretty girl who always had a smile for Rashawn. She had once helped to save the Black Dinosaurs when they were trapped in an underground tunnel. Mimi, a petite, coffee-cheeked girl with long black braids, "ate math problems for breakfast," her classmates said. She never got anything less than an A in any math class and had already skipped to the seventh-grade book.

Liza was the fastest runner in the school, and everyone knew that she could also beat up any kid in the school—boy or girl. She smiled easily and would give her last gummy bear to a friend, but she had a quick temper and had once broken a window with her fist. Her best friend, Brandy, wrote poetry. She always carried a pencil and paper with her to jot down ideas. Brandy had a fondness for jelly beans and always kept some in her book bag.

"Is everyone here?" asked the bus driver.

Rico looked at Jerome and started to say, "Ziggy—" when a police siren screaming in the distance pierced the silence of the morning. Everyone in the parking lot turned to look as the sound of the siren got closer. Speeding around the corner, a police car suddenly roared into the parking lot, with lights flashing, siren blaring, and Rashawn and Ziggy waving from the two back windows.

Everyone cheered and crowded around the police car, which was driven by Rashawn's dad. Rashawn was proud that his dad was a cop, and even prouder that he had broken the rules to drive them to the parking lot in such a blaze of glory.

"Thanks, Dad," he whispered. His dad put his arm around Rashawn and smiled.

POLICE ☎ 911   105

92P28J

POLIC

Ziggy got out of the police car slowly, grinning and waving to the cheering crowd of his friends. "Not to worry, mon! Ziggy is here!" he said dramatically. He was dressed in his favorite red jeans and a huge purple coat that came almost to the tops of his new green tennis shoes. The coat had belonged

to Ziggy's cousin and was filled with large pockets, small pockets, zippers, and flaps.

"Where's your backpack, Ziggy?" asked Rico. "It's right here, mon," replied Ziggy with a grin, pointing to his coat. "I've got socks in this pocket, a clean T-shirt here, and a peanut-butter-and-pickle sandwich in this one! Everything a mon needs for a camping trip is right here in my coat pockets!"

Noni, the counselor from Camp Caesar, dressed in the light brown uniform of the Ohio State Department of Parks and Recreation, looked tanned and tough. She wore her hair in one long black braid tied with a piece of leather in the back.

"She looks like an Indian maiden," Tiana whispered to Mimi.

Noni checked her list and announced loudly, "Campers, load the bus now. Stow your gear in the overhead racks. Let's head out of here!"

Rico's mom gave him a quick hug and a final warning: "Be careful, now! Have fun!" Rico wondered how he could do both, but he just nodded and ran to the bus.

Rashawn got his gear from the back of the police car, gave a last wave to his dad, and headed for the bus. "See you tomorrow, Dad! Don't tell Mom I left my winter coat in your car!"

His dad grinned. "I don't think you'll need it. Go on and don't worry about it. She worries enough for the three of us!" Rashawn gave his father a look of thanks and stomped his heavy army boots cheerfully onto the bus.

Ziggy was the last to board the bus. His purple coat flapped behind him in the early morning breeze as he jogged around the parking lot one last time.

"Let's go, Ziggy," called Noni. "Where's your sleeping bag?"

Ziggy stopped suddenly. "Oh, no!" he exclaimed. "I left it at home, mon! I was so excited about riding in the police car that I forgot it. Let's see, I hugged my mum, put my hat on, fed my cat on the front porch—it's on my porch!"

Noni sighed, looked at her watch, and said, "Well, Ziggy . . ."

Just then Ziggy's mom pulled into the parking lot.

His face brightened as he ran to the car. She shook her head as if to say, *When will you learn, Ziggy?* but she smiled, knowing it wouldn't be the last time he'd forget and she would have to bail him out. She had brought his costume to school on the day of the class play, and his tie on the day of the vocal music concert.

"Oh thanks, Mum! You're the best! I promise I'll never do this again! Not to worry!" He hugged her through the car window, kissed her on the cheek, and leaped onto the bus. He waved and grinned at her from the window and blew her another kiss. She couldn't help laughing.

Finally, Noni told the driver to close the doors and take off. Everyone cheered as the bus roared out of the parking lot, leaving the parents waving behind it.

As the bus lumbered down the highway, the signs and sights of the city began to disappear. Trees and fields and cows soon replaced houses and stores and people.

"Look, mon!" cried Ziggy as he looked out of the window of the bus. "A deer! With antlers! Oh, wow! There's three—no, four—wait! I see six of them!" Everyone crowded to Ziggy's side of the bus to see. The small herd of deer looked up briefly, then darted into the thick woods behind them. *It's gonna be a good trip,* thought Ziggy with satisfaction as he settled back into his seat.

The ride from their school to Caesar's Creek State Park took only about forty-five minutes. Before they knew it, the bus was turning down a small road. Straight ahead the children could see a large brown sign that read: CAESAR CREEK STATE PARK— 5 MILES.

Ziggy bounced on his seat with excitement. Rico looked at Jerome and grinned. Rashawn looked at Tiana, but she was busy looking out of the window, or at least she pretended to be.

"Hey, Noni!" Ziggy yelled from the back of the bus. "How come we got a park in Ohio named for Julius Caesar? Did he sleep here or something?"

"I'm glad you asked that, Ziggy," Noni replied with a smile. "Everyone listen up!" The bus got quiet for a moment, and Noni stood in the middle of the aisle, swaying with the bus as it twisted its way down the narrow roads that led to the camp. She asked loudly, "Does anyone know where Caesar's Creek got its name?"

"Julius Caesar fell into a creek here?" Rashawn asked. Tiana giggled.

"Nope," Noni said, shaking her head.

"Julius Caesar discovered it?" asked Mimi.

"Not even close!" Noni chuckled. "As a matter of fact, it wasn't named for Julius Caesar at all! Any more guesses?"

"Maybe it was named for Caesar's wife!" exclaimed Liza. The girls all laughed and agreed.

"Sorry, girls," Noni replied. "That's not it either."

"So who was it named for, Noni?" asked Jerome.

"Listen!" she began. The bus had slowed to a stop. "Caesar's Creek really was named for a man named Caesar. And this Caesar was a mighty, mighty man." She paused for a moment.

Ziggy had moved several seats closer so he could hear Noni better. He loved stories about heroes.

Noni continued, the excitement building in her voice as she watched the faces of the children on the bus. "Caesar was a black man—an African American, an ex-slave, an explorer, and an Indian chief. And this was *his* valley, land given to him by the Shawnee Indians!"

She waved her arms and pointed toward the thick greenery all around them. At that, the door of the bus opened.

"Awesome, mon!" whispered Ziggy as he jumped from the top step of the bus to the gravel-covered parking lot. "Awesome!"

 **Three**

The bus was finally unloaded and everyone stood blinking in the bright sunlight, quiet for a moment, looking up at the tall trees and into the shadows of the deep green forest in the distance. Birds chirped, the trees swayed in the soft breeze, and squirrels chased each other on the thin branches. Fifty feet from where they stood, a small pond rippled slightly in the morning sunshine.

"Looks like a postcard!" whispered Mimi. "It's so quiet and pretty!"

"And *all* of this belonged to this dude named Caesar?" asked Rashawn in amazement. "How did he get here? Where did he come from? And why did the Shawnees give it to him?"

"I'll answer all of your questions tonight at the campfire," Noni promised. "But first we have to get settled at our campsite."

"Where's our cabins, Noni?" asked Brandy. "It's pretty out here, but all I see is forest!"

"Sorry, Brandy," Noni answered, "no cabins for this trip. We're going to pitch our tents and sleep in the open air!"

"Cool!" she replied. "Maybe I'll write a poem about the 'murky midnight air'!"

"Open air!" gasped Jerome. "You mean where bugs can crawl on you at night?"

"Bugs gotta sleep too, mon!" Ziggy offered. "Not to worry!"

Noni decided it was time to show them a little nature up close. "Come over here," she said as she walked to the pond. They followed as she walked to the edge of the pond, near the tall, reedy plants that grew in the water. "I want you to tell me what you see."

"I see water," said Tiana. "And look! I can see your reflection, Rico. Yours, too, Rashawn," she added shyly.

"I see bushes growing in the water," added Brandy.

"And leaves floating on the water—almost like they were growing there!" observed Mimi.

"You're right," said Noni, smiling. "Those are water lilies. Keep looking."

"I see bugs flying real close to the water—they look like little dive-bombers!" said Jerome as he watched them. "They don't look so bad."

"There's a little fish in the water too!" cried Rico. "Look! There's a whole bunch of them!"

"I don't see anything, mon!" moaned Ziggy. Suddenly he jumped up and cried, "I see a frog! It's green and fat and I bet I can catch it!" Just as he lunged for the frog, Noni caught him by the tail of his purple coat.

"Not so fast, Ziggy!" she warned. "What are you going to do if you catch it?"

"Uh, I'll put it in a jar—or a cage—or, I don't know, just keep it, mon!"

"And then what?" Noni asked gently.

"I'll feed it!" Ziggy replied.

"What do frogs eat?" Noni continued.

"Worms, I guess—and bugs! Hundreds of them!" Ziggy said firmly.

"And you're going to catch hundreds of bugs and worms for your frog every day?" The other kids were beginning to smile.

"Hundreds?"

"Frogs get very hungry," Noni explained with a grin.

"Well, maybe I'll just let this little frog catch his own dinner tonight, mon," admitted Ziggy. "But I could have caught him if I wanted to!" Everyone laughed as the frog jumped with a huge splash into the water just at that moment.

"Okay, everyone," called Noni, "grab your gear and let's head for the campsite. We've got a long walk, then we have to set up our tents." The campers all groaned, but they gathered their packs and bags and followed Noni down a path into the woods.

"How far is it?" asked Rashawn after only a few minutes. "It seems so different from when we're at home and walking around the neighborhood."

"Just a couple of miles," replied Noni cheerfully. "Don't worry about the distance—just look around you as we walk and check out *my* neighborhood!"

The woods were much cooler and darker than the bright, sunny pond they had just left. Above them the sky was sometimes completely hidden by dark green leaves. Crunchy pine needles and old, fallen leaves covered the path they followed.

Jerome took off his sunglasses and tucked them into his backpack. He, Rico, and Rashawn all wore

hiking boots. But Ziggy wore his bright green tennis shoes. The soles were soft, and along with the sounds of the birds and the crickets Ziggy's "OUCH, MON!" echoed through the forest.

Liza was the only one who really seemed to enjoy the hike. She kept up with Noni and breathed deeply the fresh outdoor air. Brandy seemed to enjoy it too, but she was looking at the woods and birds for ideas, not for exercise. She gobbled jelly beans as they walked, dropping a few every now and then. Tiana stayed either just in front of or just behind Rashawn, but he pretended to ignore her.

Noni walked slowly, pointing out the names of

trees as they followed—oak, maple, birch, elm, and more. She showed them owl and deer droppings and told them how they could tell the difference and what they could learn about an animal from their droppings.

"Yuck!" squealed Tiana. "That's disgusting!"

"Everything's gotta poop, mon!" Ziggy explained cheerfully. "What's the big deal?"

"You're gross, Ziggy!" Brandy accused. He just laughed, ran off the path, and bumped into a tree. His long purple coat had gotten too warm, so he tied it around his waist by the sleeves. He spotted a leafy green plant next to him, so he broke off a piece and offered it to Brandy.

"Here!" he teased. He bowed like he had seen men do in movies and offered her the plant as if it were a beautiful bouquet. "Write something beautiful about my green gift!"

Noni turned around and yelled, "Ziggy! Throw that down! It's poison ivy!"

Ziggy tossed the plant into the trees and screamed. "I touched it! I'm gonna die, mon!" He fell to the ground, rolled on his back, and kicked his arms and legs.

Noni laughed and shook her head. "Is he always like this?" she asked the rest of the kids.

"He's usually worse!" Rico replied as he grinned at Ziggy.

Noni got Ziggy up, brushed the leaves off his clothes, and washed his hands off with an alcohol wipe. "You might get a rash, Ziggy, but there's a chance you won't have any reaction at all."

"How do we know if it's poison ivy?" asked Jerome. "All this stuff looks the same to me."

"Poison ivy has clusters of three leaves. Try to remember this little rhyme: 'Leaves of three, watch out for me.'"

Ziggy was much quieter now. He stayed on the path right behind Noni. He kept looking at his hands.

"Whatcha doin'?" asked Rico.

"I'm checking to see if my hands are gonna fall off, mon!"

Noni gave Ziggy a hug. "You'll be fine. 'Not to worry!' Isn't that what you said?"

Ziggy grinned and relaxed a little. But he still checked his hands when Noni wasn't looking.

"What's that plant, Noni?" Mimi asked, pointing to a large, leafy plant growing close to the ground. "There sure is a lot of it."

"That's called a mayapple, Mimi. See this fruit growing underneath the leaves? It can be eaten, but the leaves are poisonous."

"Poisonous?" Tiana repeated.

"If you touch the leaves, like poison ivy?" asked Rico.

"No, you have to chew the leaves. I'm told they are very bitter. You'd never eat them by accident."

"Who would want to do that?" Brandy asked. She had started on her second bag of jelly beans.

"The stories say that the Indians around here would chew the leaves of the mayapple if they got captured by the settlers," Noni explained.

"I would *hate* to be captured!" Rashawn exclaimed. "To be tied up or locked up would be awful!"

"Kinda like Ziggy's frog, huh?" Tiana replied.

"Right."

"Can you imagine what it was like a long time ago when the Indians lived here?" Tiana spoke softly, looking at the quiet beauty around her. "It's so pretty!"

"And a little scary, too!" Mimi added.

"I can almost feel the shadows of the Indians who walked here a long time ago," Brandy said dramatically.

"I would love to have been an Indian boy!" Rico said strongly. "Just hunting and fishing and playing in the woods all day!"

"I wonder if Indian boys ever got poison ivy, mon," Ziggy said quietly. He had started to scratch his left arm.

 **Four**

They walked through the woods slowly, looking at birds and flowers that Noni pointed out, laughing and shouting at one another.

"You'd never make it as young Indians," Noni told them with a laugh. "You're much too noisy! A young Shawnee boy could walk through the deepest part of these woods and never even snap a twig!"

"Well, Shawnee boys didn't wear hiking boots like Jerome," Mimi answered.

"Or bright green tennis shoes like Ziggy!" added Brandy.

"I'm gonna pretend I'm an Indian brave," declared Jerome.

"Well, you better go catch that squirrel for dinner, mon!" teased Ziggy.

"I'm getting hungry, Noni," complained Rico. "When can we eat? Are we almost there?"

"Look!" Noni pointed with pride.

The path had widened, and the trees disappeared behind them. The children stopped suddenly, amazed and silenced by what they saw. They stood at the edge of a huge meadow. The bright sun, after the dim shadows of the woods, made the meadow shine with a golden glow. A path had been broken through the tall grasses. At the end of the path on the other side of the meadow lay a large blue lake.

"Wow!" exclaimed Rashawn. "Cool!"

"It's beautiful," Tiana remarked with a smile.

Brandy stopped eating her jelly beans long enough to pull out her notebook. She scribbled a few words, then stood silently, breathing deeply of the sweet, crisp air.

Ziggy didn't have time for poetic moments. He

rushed past the rest of them and ran down the path toward the lake. "Whoopee!" he cried. "Let's go fishing!"

"You probably scared away every fish for a hundred miles," called Noni. "Let's get these tents up first. We'll set them up in this clearing—girls' tent over here, boys' tent over there. We'll make our campfire in the middle."

Noni had been carrying the two tents on her pack. She showed them how easy it was to change the small folded objects into tents. Rashawn and Jerome helped her with the stakes, while Mimi and Tiana pulled and wrapped the rope. Rico and Ziggy went to collect twigs for the fire, while Brandy and Liza unrolled the sleeping bags and unpacked the food.

"Where are you gonna sleep, Noni?" Liza asked.

"Since this is the larger tent, I'll sleep with the girls, of course," she replied.

"Well, who's gonna protect *us*?" Jerome inquired. "Suppose a bear comes and kidnaps us while you're sleeping?"

"You've got Ziggy," Noni replied with a laugh. "No bear would dare bother you!"

Ziggy and Rico returned just then. Each carried an armload of sticks. "What's so funny, mon?" Ziggy asked with a grin.

"Oh, nothing," said Mimi, giggling. "Just thinking about what Ziggybear soup might taste like!"

"Yummy, of course, mon!" Ziggy laughed as he dumped the pile of sticks right near Mimi's foot.

"Sorry, no Ziggybear soup today," said Noni, "but let's eat lunch. You all have worked very hard this morning."

"All right!" cheered Rashawn. He pulled a large, overstuffed brown paper lunch bag out of his backpack. He dumped the contents on the grass in front of him—a bag of potato chips, three cheese sandwiches, an apple, an orange, a large plastic bottle of juice, and six chocolate cookies.

"How many did you pack for, Rashawn?" asked Rico. "You got enough there for an army."

"It will take an army to get it from me," mumbled Rashawn as he bit into the apple. "I'm hungry!"

"Do you want to trade one of those cheese sandwiches for my ham sandwich?" Tiana asked Rashawn.

Rashawn shook his head. His mouth was too full to reply. Jerome told her, "Naw, you keep it. He won't trade. Rashawn doesn't eat meat."

"Oh, yeah, I forgot," Tiana muttered. She felt a little embarrassed.

Rashawn grinned at her. "Don't worry about it. I'll take one of your cupcakes for a chocolate cookie, though," he said, offering it to her.

Rico and Ziggy giggled. They knew that Rashawn didn't give up his chocolate cookies for just anybody. Tiana smiled as she nibbled at the cookie.

Ziggy's lunch was a sight to behold. Each of the pockets of the purple coat held something different. First he pulled out his peanut-butter-and-pickle sandwich and set it in front of him. From another pocket he pulled a grapefruit. From a pocket with a zipper came a bottle of juice—prune juice. In a large, buttoned pocket, wrapped in foil, he had hidden four large pancakes. Two were covered with

jelly; two were covered with ketchup. Finally, he pulled what looked like the largest piece of fried chicken ever seen out of the final pocket.

"What is *that*?" hooted Liza. "Fried chicken for a giant?"

"No, mon," replied Ziggy with fake dignity as he bit into it. "It's fried turkey. Doesn't everybody eat at Kentucky Fried Turkey?"

Ziggy kept them all laughing as they finished their lunches and watched him gobble his amazing meal. Rico, Rashawn, and Jerome were used to Ziggy's unusual eating habits, but the girls couldn't believe it as Ziggy bit into the grapefruit, skin and all.

After the quick lunch cleanup, the girls wandered down to the lake. Liza took off her shoes and socks and squealed as the chilly water touched her feet. Brandy sat on the rocky beach, snacking on jelly beans and writing in her notebook. Mimi tossed stones into the water, trying to count the ripples and circles as they wobbled on the water. Tiana glanced over at the four boys to see what Rashawn was doing, but he was busy wrestling with Ziggy in the tall grass. She noticed a small canoe hidden under some bushes near the water's edge.

Tiana wandered over and helped Noni tidy up the campsite, and the two of them sat down and watched the rest of the kids.

"You've got a cool job, Noni," Tiana said as she looked for four-leaf clovers in the grass.

"I love my job," Noni replied with enthusiasm. "Every weekend I get to take small groups of children to the woods and let them explore and discover the beauty of nature. I get to take young people like you away from the other side of the park, where it's so crowded with motor homes and portable televisions. This is the real deal."

They chuckled at the four boys, who were pretending to be Indian braves on a hunt. They shot imaginary arrows from invisible bows, running through the tall grasses of the meadow, darting into the shadows of the trees to hide.

"I got that moose, mon!" shouted Ziggy.

"Moose?" asked Jerome. "Why not a squirrel or a rabbit?"

"When Ziggy hunts, he hunts moose, mon!"

Rico was on his knees, digging in the soft soil of the meadow. "Look at this funny rock, Rashawn. It's pointed, and it's such an odd color."

Rashawn looked up from where he had been sitting under a tall pine tree, pretending not to watch Tiana, who had joined the other girls by the water. "Let me see it." The rock was dirty, but was very light in color. "Let's take it down to the water and rinse it off."

"I'll race you!" yelled Rico as he sprinted across the meadow. Rashawn's long legs soon caught and passed Rico. Jerome and Ziggy raced also, but Jerome won easily because Ziggy's purple coat got wrapped around his legs and slowed him down.

Rico took the rock down to the water's edge and carefully washed it off. He rubbed the dirt with his fingers and with a soft stick he'd found. His heart began to beat faster. "I think I've found something really cool," he whispered.

No one heard him, because Rashawn had dumped a handful of cold lake water down Tiana's back, and she screamed and ran down the small, rocky beach. Mimi and Brandy had grabbed Jerome and were trying to pull him into the water. He was strong enough to shake them off, but when Liza headed over to join them, he broke free of the girls and ran laughing in the other direction.

Rico called to Ziggy, who was running toward the girls. "Look, Ziggy—what do you think this is?"

Ziggy took the small, clean stone from Rico's hand. But it wasn't a rock. It was clear like a crystal—he could see the palm of his hand beneath it. It was shaped like a small pine tree, sharply pointed, with sharp edges on each side.

"Hey, mon," whispered Ziggy with respect. "I think you have found a real live Indian arrowhead!"

Five

"**Let's go see if we can find some more arrow-**heads!" Rico shouted. He and Ziggy ran over to the spot where Rico had been digging. They dug furiously with their fingers and hands in the soft, black dirt, but all they found were dirty old rocks and worms.

"Who do you think it belonged to?" Rico asked as he wiped the dirt off his hands and looked down at the clear, shining arrowhead.

"I think it's pretty special, mon," Ziggy replied. "Most arrowheads are made of stone or some sort of rock. This one almost looks like a crystal."

"Should we show Noni?" Rico asked.

"Let's wait, mon," Ziggy suggested. "Let's just wait a bit."

Rico agreed and put the arrowhead carefully into his pocket. They walked back down to the beach where Noni was showing the girls how to put a worm on a hook to fish.

"EEEK!" screamed Mimi. "It jumped out of my hand! Now I don't have to do this."

Rico ran over and picked up the worm. "Here, Mimi," he said with a grin. "I think you dropped your worm." He smashed the worm into her hand. She screamed again and threw it at him. Rico chuckled and ducked.

Liza had baited her own hook and now stared at the water, waiting for a bite. "Shhh!" she whispered fiercely. "You'll chase away my fish."

Ziggy and Rico called to Rashawn and Jerome, and the four boys walked down the beach a little ways from where the girls were fishing. "We got something to show you, mon," Ziggy told them.

Rico pulled the arrowhead out of his pocket and showed them.

"It's quartz," stated Jerome. "That was a very special arrowhead—used for special occasions or special people."

"How do you know so much?" asked Rashawn.

"Don't you remember? I did a report in school last year on Native Americans. I remember what I read about the arrowheads because I thought it would be really cool to find one," Jerome explained. "What are you going to do with it?"

"I don't know yet," Rico admitted. "I have a feeling there's something *very* special about this." They all agreed.

"Let's ask Noni what she knows about the Native Americans who used to live here," Jerome suggested.

"Yeah, mon, and she's got to tell us about the dude named Caesar, too," added Ziggy.

"I think she knows a lot," Rico said. "Doesn't she look a little like an Indian to you?"

"Just because she's got long black hair doesn't make her Indian. She looks Black to me," commented Rashawn.

"I thought she was Chinese, mon!" Ziggy

exclaimed. "What difference does it make? I'm hungry!"

By the time everyone finished fishing, the shadows of the evening were beginning to darken the skies over the lake. Mimi had caught six fish— more than anybody—and she carried them proudly back to the camp with the others.

The neat pile of sticks over a circle of rocks was ready to become their campfire. Noni said, "Come and look closely. I'm going to show you a very special method of starting a fire."

"You gonna rub two sticks together?" Rico asked.

"No, you gotta rub a stone and a flint," said Jerome with authority.

"No, that's not it," Noni said with a little mystery in her voice. "Are you ready? Here is it is!"

Tiana gasped as Noni pulled out a book of matches. Everybody groaned and laughed. Noni started the fire and showed them how to keep it safe. It sparkled and crackled with bright orange fire.

"Let's fry this fish now," she said as she pulled a pan out of her pack.

"We're gonna eat dead fish, mon?" asked Ziggy.

Mimi laughed. "No, Ziggy," she teased. "We're gonna eat live fish instead!"

"Well, that's better!" Ziggy replied.

Noni just shook her head at Ziggy as she showed them how to prepare and cook the fish they had caught. The sizzling smell of frying fish made the campers realize how hungry they were. Noni added some sliced potatoes and onions, and dinner was ready in no time. Cold water from their canteens topped off the meal.

"Delicious!" Ziggy burped as he finished the last of his dinner.

"I'd never eat this at home," admitted Liza. "But it was really good."

"Thanks," Noni replied. "I'm glad you liked it. Now let's get this stuff cleaned up."

Everyone pitched in. Rashawn collected the paper plates and cups and tossed them into a trash bag, while Tiana collected all of the rest of the trash. Liza and Brandy gathered more sticks and branches for the fire, and Ziggy and Rico ran down to the edge of the lake to wash the pan. Jerome followed them with the plastic forks.

"Look, mon!" cried Ziggy. "I wonder who owns that canoe."

"I know how to paddle a canoe," Rico boasted. "My dad taught me last summer when I went to visit him."

"I wish we could try it out, mon," Ziggy said wistfully. "It looks like it's been hidden here awhile. Do you think Noni knows it's here?"

"Probably not," Jerome figured. "Look how old it is. It hasn't been used for a very long time."

"Let's get back," Rico suggested. "We'll check it out in the morning."

Darkness was falling quickly. The fire at the campsite looked bright and inviting. The boys raced back to it as the shadows of the evening became the blackness of night.

"Gather around the fire," Noni called. "Bring your sleeping bags to sit on. I've got a story to tell you!"

Jerome, Ziggy, and Rico sat together on Rico's bag. Mimi sat next to Noni, while Liza and Brandy sat on the other side of the circle. The only space left was next to Tiana, so Rashawn plopped down beside her. She smiled shyly. His look told the boys they'd better not dare tease him. Ziggy rolled on the sleeping bag, hands covering his mouth, trying not to burst out laughing.

The fire at the middle of their circle was warm and cheerful. Beyond it lay only darkness. Everyone stared at it for a few moments, watching it eat the sticks and branches with a bright red sizzle and pop.

"Tell us about Caesar," Mimi whispered.

"A long time ago," Noni began quietly, "no one lived in what we know as the Ohio Valley except for Native Americans. This was their land, and they roamed from the lakes to the forests and beyond, hunting only what they needed to eat, living in harmony with the land and the animals. The air was clean, the waters were blue, and nature was respected by the people who lived in it and loved it.

"About three hundred years ago, European settlers began to arrive here. Their way of life was very different. They destroyed the forests to build houses and towns. They built large farms on which they grew crops to buy and sell. And instead of trying to live *with* the Native Americans, they chased them out of their own land."

Rashawn tossed a stick into the fire, a frown on his face. "We studied about this in school," he said. "The Indians got treated really dirty."

"Didn't the Indians fight back?" asked Rico.

"I've seen movies about the settlers and the Indians on TV," Liza said. "Usually the settlers win."

"Yeah, I've seen movies where it seems like one

bullet from a settler's gun kills about five Indians," added Rashawn.

"It was a terrible time," Noni continued. "Thousands of people died from both cultures. Many of the government policies about the Indians were unfair and cruel. Hatred and sorrow seemed to rule."

"Speaking of hatred and sorrow, wasn't this about the same time that slavery started?" asked Jerome. "We learned about that in school too."

"You're right," Noni said with a sigh. "Black people from Africa were being brought here as slaves to work on the huge farms in the South."

"Why didn't they make the Indians be slaves?" Tiana asked.

"Well, they tried. But the Native Americans lived here and knew the land and forests well. They could escape and never be found because they had friends nearby who spoke their language and who could help them. Black people looked different and were easily spotted. And they had no one to help them, except . . ."

Noni paused to make sure everyone was listening. The fire crackled and insects chirped in the distance.

"Except who, mon?" Ziggy interrupted.

". . . except the Indians!" Noni concluded dramatically.

"Indians?" Brandy asked. "Why would they help runaway slaves?"

"They probably thought it was cool to upset the slave owners," Liza said.

"Yeah, and they probably wanted to help anybody who was being mistreated even worse than they were," added Mimi.

"You're both right," Noni admitted. "Thousands of runaway slaves were helped by Native Americans. But there's more."

"So tell us, mon!" Ziggy insisted. He loved stories with secrets.

"Many of the runaways stayed with the Indians. They were accepted and adopted into the Indian tribes and became part of their families."

"Awesome!" declared Rashawn.

"How come that wasn't in the books when I did my report on Native Americans last year?" asked Jerome.

"There's quite a bit that's sometimes left out of history books," Noni admitted. "This is just another fact of history that's often overlooked."

"Yeah, like this Caesar dude, mon," added Ziggy. "If he was so great and got a park named after him, how come we never heard of him?"

"And how come you know so much about him?" Brandy asked.

"Caesar was my great-great-grandfather," Noni responded softly.

Six

"**Wow!**" **Liza exclaimed.** "**Why didn't you tell us?**"

"You didn't ask," Noni said with a smile.

"He was a slave, right?" Jerome asked.

"Yes. From what we know, he was a harness maker and blacksmith in Maryland. His master brought him on a trip to this area sometime around 1775."

"Gee, that was the year of the start of the Revolutionary War," Mimi remembered.

"Right. Americans fought for freedom in that war, but not freedom for slaves. It took another hundred years for that," Noni added.

"But what about Caesar, mon? Finish the story!" cried Ziggy impatiently.

"Okay, Ziggy," Noni responded. "We're not sure, but Caesar may have escaped from his owner while he was here, or another story says his owner was killed."

"I bet he saw this valley and just took off!" said Rico.

"The Shawnee Indians found him hiding in the woods and took him to their village. They fed him and gave him a warm and safe place to sleep," Noni continued.

"I wonder if he was scared," Mimi said.

"He was probably so happy to be safe and free that he didn't have time to be scared!" Liza answered.

"Caesar found a safe haven with the Shawnee Indians. They taught him their language and how to find food as well as joy in the forest."

"They saved his life," Jerome said. "Awesome."

"Yes," Noni acknowledged. "But in a way, Caesar saved their lives as well."

"How?" asked Brandy. She was gobbling jelly beans again.

"Caesar was a harness maker. He knew how to make belts and harnesses and ropes from leather, and how to connect buckles to hold them. The Indian harnesses were thin and broke easily. When they went into battle, sometimes they lost control of their horses because of the weak harnesses."

"They would fall off?" asked Mimi.

"With a thud!" answered Noni.

"Ouch!"

"Many times the harnesses were so weak," Noni added with a chuckle, "the only reason the Indians didn't fall off was because they had such a strong bond with their horses."

"I bet I could ride a horse bareback!" boasted Rico.

"And I bet he'd throw you on your bare back, mon!" Ziggy teased.

Noni continued, "Anyway, Caesar taught the Indians how to make tight leather harnesses with buckles for their horses. It really made a difference. In addition, he was wise and kind, and they loved him for his gentle spirit."

"So that's why the Shawnees gave him the land?" asked Liza.

"Yes, they first found him by a creek that they named Caesar's Creek. And when they gave him this valley as a token of their appreciation for him, hundreds and hundreds of beautiful acres, this whole area became known as the Caesar's Creek area."

"I thought you said he was an Indian chief," declared Rashawn.

"Yes, he was!" Noni replied proudly. "He stayed with the Shawnee for the rest of his life. He married a Shawnee woman and had several children. Later he was placed in charge of several other families and rose to the rank of subchief, second only to the principal chief of the tribe."

"Wow!"

"Do you think he could make arrowheads?" Rico asked.

"Sure, Rico," Noni answered. "He probably used quartz tips, since he was a chief. Why do you ask?"

Rico and Ziggy looked at each other and grinned.

"Oh, no special reason," Rico said quickly. "Do you think there are any arrowheads around here? It would be cool to find one."

"It's possible to find flint arrowheads, but quartz tips are very rare and special," Noni replied. "Indian boys about your age were taught to make tips for their arrows by the older men of the tribe."

"What was it like for Indian kids our age?" Jerome asked.

"All children were loved and adored. Every adult in the tribe helped care for and discipline the children, so it was like one big family."

"Did the girls get stuck doing dumb stuff like sewing and cooking?" asked Liza.

"The women and girls usually took care of making the clothes and preparing the food, yes, but they also had power in the tribal council and could even be chief."

"Well, I guess that makes me feel a little better," Liza said, "but could girls go hunting for game?"

"Yes, they could. Many of the women were expert

hunters—some could even outshoot the men," Noni informed her.

"Cool!"

"What about the boys?" asked Rico. "Didn't they have to do mighty deeds to prove their courage and stuff?"

"You're right, Rico," Noni responded, "the boys did have manhood ceremonies. *Really* cool stuff."

Ziggy stood up and raised his fists like a warrior. "That's me, mon! Cool Indian brave!"

The girls rolled their eyes at Ziggy's boasting. Noni smiled halfheartedly and whispered to Liza and Brandy, "Watch this!"

"Okay, Ziggy," Noni called, "would you like to demonstrate one of the Shawnee ceremonies that boys did to prove their manhood?"

"Yeah, mon!" Ziggy jumped and danced around the fire, copying movies he had seen on TV.

Noni explained, "Every boy in the tribe, at the age of eight, had to take a walk every morning."

"I can do that!" Ziggy declared. "No problem, mon!"

"They had to walk to the river."

"No problem!"

"Every morning for three months."

"No problem!"

"Did I mention the three months were December, January, and February?"

"No problem! I'd wear a coat!"

"Did I mention that at the end of the walk, the boy had to jump in the river?"

"No problem! Uh, wouldn't my shoes and coat get wet?"

Noni was about to pop with laughter. "Did I mention that the boy took this walk every morning in the snow with no shoes?"

"No prob—uh, no shoes?"

"Did I mention that the boy took this walk every morning and then jumped into the frozen river *with no clothes on*?"

"No way, mon!" Ziggy sat back down in a hurry and shivered. The girls were rolling with laughter.

"Really cool manhood stuff, Ziggy!" teased Tiana. "So cool you'd be frozen!"

Noni laughed too. "You know, people still talk about when the great Shawnee warrior Tecumseh was a boy and had to do his challenge in the snow."

"I know about Tecumseh!" Brandy exclaimed. "We read about him in school. What did he do for his challenge?"

"Tecumseh walked naked in the snow in the coldest winter ever known; the water was frozen most mornings and had to be broken for him so he could jump in."

"Ouch! Maybe I'm not ready to be a warrior just yet, mon," Ziggy admitted. "Were there any easier tests?" he asked with a grin.

"There were other manhood tests as well, and special challenges for the young girls, also," Noni answered. "The young people would have to go on trips alone, sometimes in the woods at night, sometimes on the water, sometimes to the Great House, which was their place of the spirit."

"Look at the moon," Brandy said suddenly. Above, the moon was bright and golden—a full moon. It shone on the dark, still water of the lake in the distance, shimmering like candlelight.

"A mystery moon," Noni whispered. "Strange events will happen tonight! Shadows walk in the moonlight."

Seven

"**What do you mean, 'strange events'?**" asked Mimi. She looked up at the moon and back into the flames of the sparkling fire.

"And what kind of shadows will walk?" added Brandy. Tiana shivered and moved a fraction closer to Rashawn.

Noni's face looked dark and mysterious. Her voice was low and scary as she whispered again, "Shadows walk in the moonlight!"

"You mean like ghosts?" asked Rico.

"You trying to scare us, mon?" Ziggy asked. "'Cause you might be doing a good job!"

"There are spirits everywhere," Noni continued. "Spirits of the past, and spirits of hope, and spirits of those who once walked this land. Are you brave enough to sleep in the darkness with the shadows of the past?"

"You can't scare us!" boasted Rashawn. "We're ready to go to sleep without any flashlights, even!"

"No problem, mon!" Ziggy added.

Jerome said boldly, "Bring on all your ghosts and shadows and spirits. We're the Black Dinosaurs! We're not scared of anything!"

Rico joined them as they stood and marched to their tent, but he looked scared. They could hear Noni and the girls laughing behind them.

"Dumb girls!" Rico said. "They got Noni to protect them, though."

"We don't need anybody, mon," Ziggy boasted. "She was just trying to scare us. That's what you're supposed to do to kids on a campout!"

They crawled into their sleeping bags, which fit snugly into the tent. Each boy had a flashlight. "Ready to zip the tent?" Jerome asked.

"Ready, mon!"

"Let her zip!" added Rico.

"Now, flashlights off!" commanded Rashawn.

The darkness was almost total. They could see faint shadows from the light of the fading campfire. The light of the moon cast an eerie glow.

"You scared?" asked Rico.

"Not really," Rashawn replied, but his voice was a little shaky.

"Me neither," said Jerome. "I just hope there's no bugs crawling around inside this sleeping bag!"

"Where's the arrowhead, Rico?" Ziggy asked.

"Right here in my pocket. You know," Rico added, "I wish we could do one of those manhood tests Noni talked about."

"Like jumping naked in a frozen lake, mon? You must be nuts!"

"No, I mean like going on a night hike or searching for secrets in the stars."

"We *could* go on a hike tonight," Rashawn suggested quietly.

"Noni would never allow it," Rico declared.

"Noni would never know!" Rashawn replied excitedly. "We'll wait until she's asleep."

"You mean sneak out, mon? Awesome!"

"We'll get in really big trouble!"

"Only if we get caught!"

"How could they catch us? We'll be back in an hour!"

"Let's prove we're men, and not boys!"

"It's dark!"

"We've got flashlights."

"What about the bugs?"

"We'll take bug spray."

"Let's do it!"

"Yeah, mon! Let's do it!"

They whispered excitedly for the next hour, listening for the sounds from the girls' tent to disappear. They planned to walk down to the beach by the lake and sit in the moonlight, pretending to be Shawnee boys on a night journey. If Noni woke up and found them, they decided to tell her they had gone out to go to the bathroom.

The night finally became silent. Rashawn unzipped

the tent and listened. They could hear insects and frogs, but the girls' tent was quiet. They waited another half hour, just to make sure, then slipped quietly, one by one, out of the tent and down the path to the lake.

The night air was chilly, and Rashawn wished he had taken his mother's advice and brought his coat. The moon glowed huge and bright, lighting the water. As the four boys sat on the banks of Caesar Creek Lake, they thought silently of Indians, and adventures, and secrets of the past.

"This is cool!" Rashawn exclaimed.

"Awesome!" added Jerome.

Ziggy wore his long, purple, many-pocketed coat. He and Rico walked down the beach, scuffing their shoes in the rocky sand, and almost bumped into the canoe they had discovered earlier.

"Look, mon!" Ziggy exclaimed.

"I wonder if it's any good," Rico wondered. "It's probably full of holes."

They called Jerome and Rashawn over to help them inspect the hull of the canoe. They shone their flashlights all over it, and it looked faded but surprisingly solid.

Together they pushed and pulled it right side up. It was about fifteen feet long. Two seats had been nailed across it, and two paddles were tucked neatly on each side. Inside the boat was a flat wooden board. Hand-lettered on this plank, in faded white paint, were the words BOAT FOR SALE.

"It looks like it's been waiting for us, mon," Ziggy remarked. He climbed in.

"Maybe we better not," Rico warned.

"What harm could there be?" Rashawn said. "We're only gonna sit here on the beach for a minute." He climbed in next to Ziggy.

Jerome got in next. "Come on, Rico!" he called.

Rico climbed in next to Jerome, grinning in spite of himself.

"Indian scouts, out looking for trouble!" Jerome announced. They picked up the paddles and pretended they were paddling the boat as they checked for enemies in the distance.

"Let's see if it floats," Rashawn said suddenly. He

jumped out of the canoe. The other boys jumped out too, excited because they had all had the same thought. "Come on, help me push it into the water!"

Rico didn't want to, but he helped anyway. With a huge push from the boys, the canoe slipped silently into the black water of Lake Caesar and started to float away from the shore.

"Catch it!" shouted Jerome. "If it floats away, we'll get in trouble!" He ran into the water and reached for the canoe, but he couldn't hold it alone.

"Jump in, mon!" yelled Ziggy. Rashawn grabbed for one other side of the boat as Jerome steadied the other side. Both boys pulled themselves into the bottom of the boat.

Ziggy jumped in next. Finally, Rico, who didn't want the other boys to tease him, jumped in as well. The four boys looked around.

The boat had drifted thirty feet from the shore. Slightly wet and really excited, the boys grinned with pleasure as the small canoe rocked gently in the night breeze, drifting away with each rock of the waves. The moon still shone brightly, lighting what looked like a path on the water.

"I feel like a Shawnee boy!" Rashawn said with a smile.

"On a night challenge?"

"Maybe, but this is pretty easy," Rashawn boasted.

"We better get back, mon," Ziggy suggested with regret. Rico was glad that someone else had said what he'd been thinking.

"Where are the paddles?" asked Rico.

"Uh-oh! I think we've got a small problem—no, make that a *big* problem," Jerome said softly.

"What's wrong?"

"We left the paddles onshore!"

Eight

The breeze had picked up, and as they looked back at the beach, the boys saw that the canoe had drifted almost a hundred feet from the shore. They could see in the distance the tiny faint glow of their campfire. All around them rippled the dark, silent water.

"What are we gonna do?" Rico worried. "I knew this wasn't a good idea!"

"We can't swim back to shore," said Jerome. "It's too dark and the water is too deep."

"What if we call for help?" Rashawn suggested.

"Who's gonna hear us, mon?" Ziggy moaned. "Now I really *do* have to go to the bathroom!"

The canoe bounced on the water, drifting the four friends farther and farther away from camp, and safety, and even the girls.

"Do you think Noni will get up and check on us?" Jerome asked.

"Yeah, but even if she does, where will she look for us in the middle of the night?" Rashawn answered with defeat.

"Maybe she knows about the canoe and will notice it's gone, mon. Not to worry—not to worry!" Ziggy kept repeating, but he sounded worried anyway.

"And maybe she won't notice at all," cried Rico. "We may drift here all night!"

"What would Tecumseh do?" asked Jerome. "If this was a night challenge, a young person would have to be brave and think of a solution, right?"

"Right," agreed Rashawn. "But I don't feel very brave. I'm cold, and I wish I had listened to my mother and brought my coat."

"Hey, I got an idea, mon!" Ziggy said suddenly.

"What about this 'Boat for Sale' sign? We could use it as a paddle!"

"Good idea, Ziggy!" said Jerome. "Rico, you said you knew how to paddle a canoe, right? Do your thing, man!"

Rico picked up the plank and dipped it slowly into the water. He pulled it through the water as his father had shown him. But the canoe barely moved.

"What's wrong, Rico? Why aren't we moving?" Rashawn asked.

"When I was with my dad, it was much easier," admitted Rico. "And it was daytime. And he was doing most of the paddling."

"Let's take turns, then," suggested Jerome. "Let me try."

Jerome tried paddling with the plank and agreed that it was much harder than it looked. The little canoe bobbed on the water, turning and moving a little as each boy took a turn, but it was no closer to the shore. They could no longer see even a dim spot of their campfire, and the moon had disappeared behind the clouds. Blackness surrounded them.

"We're lost."

"In the dark."

"In the middle of a lake."

"In the middle of the night."

"Not to worry, mon!" Ziggy said suddenly. "I have an idea!"

Ziggy started digging though the many pockets of his purple coat. "I know it's in here somewhere," he mumbled. Finally, he said with a shout of joy, "I found it!"

"What?" they all wanted to know.

"My umbrella, of course!" He showed them a tiny yellow and green umbrella, which, folded up, was only about five inches long.

"What good is that going to do?" asked Rashawn. "It's not raining."

"I know, mon. But look!" Ziggy pushed a button on the handle and the tiny umbrella stretched out to a full three feet long. "We can use this as a second paddle! As long as I don't push this second button to open it up, we'll be fine," he explained.

Ziggy dipped the umbrella into the water and

said to Rico, who was holding the plank, "Let's do this together, mon. Dip, push the water, up—dip, push the water, up—dip, push, up—dip, push, up."

Rico nodded in agreement, and for a few moments the sound of the two makeshift paddles splashing together in the water made them all feel better. But the canoe still wasn't moving toward the shore as they wanted. In fact, it seemed to be going in circles.

"It's not working, Ziggy," Jerome complained.

"I've got it, mon!" Ziggy shouted. "The problem is that me and Rico should be sitting next to each other, not like this! That way, we'd be rowing together and we could get this little boat back to camp. Let me just move over next to—"

"NO, ZIGGY!" they all shouted. "DON'T STAND UP!"

But it was too late. In his excitement to change places, he stood up, and the canoe started to rock. Ziggy lost his balance, fell forward, and accidentally pushed the button that made the umbrella open with a *whoosh!* The open umbrella bumped Rashawn and knocked him overboard with a splash. Ziggy tumbled

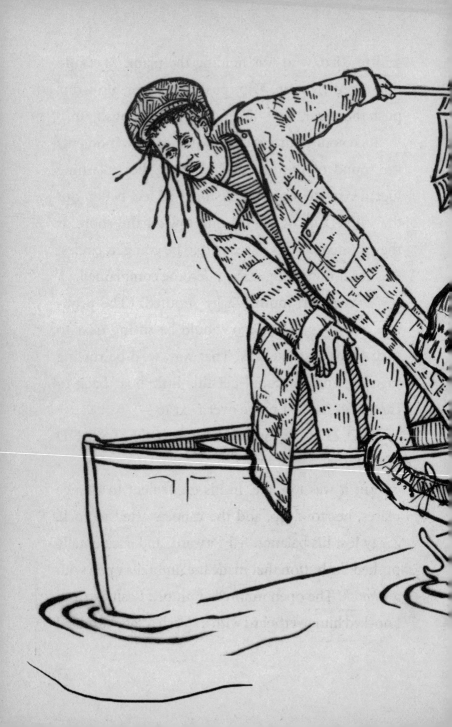

in after him, screaming. He grabbed the side of the canoe, pulled it too far, and Rico and Jerome joined them in the chilly water as the canoe tilted, filled with water, and sank with a gurgle and a thud.

The four boys were good swimmers, but the darkness and the sudden tumble into the water made everything really scary. Ziggy was screaming and splashing, trying to find the sunken canoe.

"Help! I'm drowning! It's dark out here! Where are you guys?"

"We're right here, Ziggy! Grab my hand," Jerome shouted.

"I can't find you, mon! The water is much too deep! I can't swim in the dark, mon. Help!"

Suddenly Rashawn yelled, "ZIGGY! SHUT UP AND STAND UP! We're in three feet of water! Look!"

Silence.

Then Ziggy said softly, "I knew that, mon. I was just trying to see if you had noticed." He stood up and sloshed through the shallow water to the shore.

Rico, Rashawn, and Jerome laughed in spite of themselves and followed him. Wet and cold, but glad to be safe, they sat on the sand, trying to catch their breath. "We made it," sighed Rico.

"Let's brush this sand off and head back to camp in a hurry," said Jerome. "Maybe Noni hasn't noticed that we're gone yet."

"Sand?" Rashawn said, sounding worried. He picked up handfuls of the soft white sand and let it spill through his fingers. Then he added fearfully, "There was no sand on the beach we left from. It was rocky, remember?"

"Oh, no!" Rico exclaimed. "We've landed on another beach! We must have drifted across the lake! Now we'll *never* find our way back!"

"Well, we can't stay here. We've got to keep moving so we can dry off a little and try to keep warm," declared Jerome. "Maybe our camp is not too far away." But he didn't sound very sure.

"Let's go this way," suggested Rico.

"Through the woods?" asked Rashawn.

"Why not, mon! Let's move on!" Ziggy led their way into the darkness.

They walked slowly at first, stumbling into trees and each other, bushes scratching their arms and faces. Gradually, though, the moon came from behind the clouds and they were able to make out shapes and shadows in the forest as they walked. But they were wet, cold, scared, and very, very lost.

"I wish I had a flashlight," Jerome sighed out loud.

"As long as we're wishing, mon, wish for dry clothes and a pizza!" Ziggy added.

"I wish we were back home," Rico said quietly.

"You can't have an adventure at home, Rico! Think of this as our manhood ceremony, like the Shawnee boys," Rashawn suggested as he stumbled over a vine. "The spirits of Caesar and Tecumseh are watching us. They expect us to be brave."

"I'd rather be brave in the daytime," Rico complained.

They came to a clearing. A huge log lay across one edge of this break in the thick woods. A large flat rock lay close by. Faint moonlight shone through the trees. Ziggy, Jerome, and Rico sat on the log. Rashawn stretched out on the rock. Jerome scratched his mosquito bites and checked the area for bugs as best he could in the darkness.

"Wish I had some bug spray, too," he whispered to himself.

"What should we do?" asked Rico.

"Well, we can't stay here. We've got to find our way out," Jerome replied. "The lake is a big circle.

We just walk around it until we find our camp!"

"It's a big lake," Rashawn reminded him. "And we don't even know whether to go right or left."

"I saw a movie about some kids who were lost in the woods for six weeks," Rico remembered.

"So what happened in the movie, mon?"

"The kids ate bugs and worms and leaves and stuff until they got rescued."

"Yucky, mon! Even Ziggy doesn't want to eat bugs or worms!" Ziggy replied. "Let's get out of here!"

"What would Tecumseh have done in this situation?" Rico asked thoughtfully. An owl hooted above him and he jumped.

"Tecumseh wouldn't be lost. He'd know these woods like we know the mall," Jerome replied.

"I know he wouldn't be scared. He would know how to use his head and find his way," added Rashawn.

"He'd be scared if he knew he would get in trouble when he got back, like we will, mon," Ziggy reminded them. "Noni is gonna kill us!"

"If a bear doesn't kill us first!" exclaimed Rico,

who turned with a start at the rustling noise behind them. "Did you hear that?"

"What was that noise?" Jerome whispered.

"A rabbit, maybe?" Rico offered hopefully.

"Or a bear, mon!" Ziggy said fearfully.

They heard it again, louder this time, and closer. They could hear it moving through the crunchy leaves. It seemed to be running right toward them!

"Maybe it's a lion or tiger, like you said, Ziggy," Jerome joked weakly.

"That's not funny!" Rico shouted as they started to run away from the noise.

"No, mon, I think it really *is* a bear. But whatever it is, here it comes!" Ziggy cried out.

The four boys screamed and started running wildly into the night.

Nine

Terrified of the huge black bear they were
sure was following them, the four boys crashed
noisily through the woods. Ziggy, usually the slow-
est because he liked to act silly, was in front this
time. The night breeze chilled his wet, sticky clothes,
which stuck to his body as he ran, but he didn't
even notice. He was too intent on outrunning the
bear. Rico, close behind Ziggy, tripped over a small
branch and fell forward, bumping into Ziggy in the
darkness.

Ziggy yelled over his shoulder, "You all right,
mon?"

Gasping for breath, Rico panted, "Yeah, I'm okay, just keep running! I think it's getting closer!"

Jerome and Rashawn, just a little behind Rico, yelled ahead, "We can hear the bear! It's gonna get us! Run!"

Rico yelled to the others, "Find a tree and climb it! It's our only hope of escape!"

With large, gasping breaths, Ziggy replied, "Don't you know that bears can climb trees too, mon? Just run!"

Jerome knew that bugs were biting his bare legs, which were cut and scratched from the bushes and briars. "I wish I knew where the camp was," he complained as he ran.

"We're good and lost!" gasped Jerome. "Plus I think we're going to be dinner for that bear!"

The noise in the bushes behind them got louder and closer. The animal had tracked them and was only a few feet behind them. It was just a matter of time.

Ziggy broke a speed record. He ignored branches and scratches; he didn't know where he was heading anymore. In the moonlight he could see the shadows of the trees ahead. He ran for the tree straight in front of him, hoping to try to climb it, hoping this bear didn't know it was supposed to be able to climb up after him.

Suddenly the tree moved! Standing straight and tall in front of him now were the shadows of two trees—and one of them was moving toward him.

Ziggy screamed and tried to turn, but the branches of the tall tree-shadow reached out and grabbed his wrist. Then the tree spoke to him in a powerful voice. "Where are you going in such a hurry in the middle of the night?"

By this time Rico, Rashawn, and Jerome had reached Ziggy and stopped, panting and gasping, almost too tired to scream. "Help!" breathed Rico. "A bear is chasing us!"

The shadows of the clouds moved from the moon, and for a moment the boys could see clearly. It was not a tree that held the trembling Ziggy, but a man, tall and strong. "I see no bear," he said quietly. "And all I hear is the silence of the night, that is, now that you young men are quiet. Even my ances-tors could hear all that noise you were making from miles away," he said with a chuckle.

The four friends looked at one another in amaze-ment. The night was dark, the breeze was cool, and all was silent except for the forest voices of the night.

"Who are you?" Jerome wanted to know as the man gently released Ziggy's wrists.

The man did not reply immediately, but for some reason the boys felt no threat from him.

"Where are we?" Now that the immediate danger seemed to be over, and Rashawn had started breath-ing normally again, he was ready to find out.

"Can you get us back to our camp?" asked Rico. "We're in big trouble."

"What happened to the bear, mon?" Ziggy asked finally. At that moment a large raccoon waddled slowly into the clearing. It glanced at the strange group that was disturbing its night and moved on into the forest.

"Our bear was a *raccoon*?" Rico said in disbelief. "If I wasn't so scared, that would be funny!"

"Maybe it was *makwa*, the bear, my young friend, and maybe not. Perhaps because of your fear of the darkness and your lack of knowledge about the forest, the night spirits let you *think* you heard a bear. Perhaps it was only your own fear that was chasing you."

"Could be, mon," replied Ziggy thoughtfully. "We were pretty scared."

"We're on a campout. Can you help us get back?" asked Rico, who worried enough for the four of them.

"I know that campground; it is on the other side of the lake. How did you get here?" the stranger asked.

"We found a canoe. We wanted to try a night challenge—like Shawnee boys. At first it was fun, but then the canoe started floating away, so we jumped in, and then we couldn't get back because all we had for paddles were a board and an umbrella, then our canoe turned over, and we got wet, then we were really lost and got scared and started running—and we ran into you!" explained Rico all in one breath.

"You never told us who you were, mon," said Ziggy quietly.

The stranger smiled. "My name is Hawk. Come, young friends. Let me give you food and rest. The journey back is long without a canoe, and *Keelswah*, the morning sun, will soon erase the shadows of the night. I will take you safely back to your camp."

They followed the tall, quiet stranger down a path of soft pine needles to a rough lean-to built of branches and bark. It stood close to a rock wall. A small fire burned quietly, barely disturbing the darkness; the smell of a savory soup greeted the boys, who suddenly realized just how tired and hungry they really were. From a leather bag Hawk brought out four clay bowls, which he filled with the soup and handed to each boy. He had two blankets, so he put one around Rico and Rashawn, and one around Jerome and Ziggy.

Hawk sat on a log, chuckling, watching the four boys drink the warm soup with satisfied slurps. He knew that the appetite of the young was deep as a valley, so he refilled their bowls several times. He then showed them how to rinse their bowls in a stream that the boys had not even noticed, and they drank the cold, sweet water until they were filled.

Ziggy burped, and everyone laughed. "Excuse me, mon," he said, cheerful once again. "That was a delicious meal. Even my mum couldn't beat that. Many thanks! My name is Ziggy!"

"And I'm Rico. You're a good cook. Thanks for the blankets, too. Are we far from our camp?"

"My name is Jerome," added Jerome as he offered his hand to Hawk. "Thanks for saving us."

"My name is Rashawn. You saved our lives! Do you live in these woods?"

"I only saved you from the shadows. The sunlight would have made your journey less frightening. And no, I don't live here. I love these woods—sometimes I need to feel close to the earth and I walk and camp alone for a day or two."

"Are you an Indian, mon?" Ziggy finally blurted out.

"Yes, I am," Hawk replied with quiet dignity. "I am Shawnee."

"You can't be! You wear glasses! Indians don't wear glasses!" argued Rico.

Hawk chuckled. "Sorry to disappoint you."

Jerome looked confused. "When I did my report on Indians last year, my history book said that there were no more Shawnee left in Ohio," he said. "I remember, because I wondered what had happened."

"History books do not always speak the whole truth, my son," said Hawk with a sigh. "There is much that is not said as well. Let me tell you a story."

Jerome and Rashawn sat cross-legged on the soft pine-needle floor of the lean-to, their backs against the warm stone wall. Rico and Ziggy sat close to the fire, intent on Hawk's bright, piercing eyes and wise, warm face. His hair, which was black mixed with gray, was long and tied back with a leather string. He wore dark jeans, a brown shirt, and glasses. Around his neck was a leather thong from which hung a small leather pouch. Hawk's voice was low but strong as he began his tale.

"My name is Tukemas Pope and I am chief of the Shawnee Nation of Ohio, United Remnant Band. My friends call me Hawk. We are all who are left of the millions of Shawnee who once called this land home. Our tribal lands are at a place called Shawandasse, which is not very far from here. The word *Shawandasse* means 'South Wind People.'"

"Wow! You're a chief? Should we call you 'Your Majesty'?" asked Rico.

"Goodness, no!" Hawk said, laughing. "Just call me Hawk."

"What happened to the millions of Shawnee you talked about?" Rashawn asked.

"Some were killed, some died of disease and starvation, and many died as they were forced to move from Ohio to other states. It was a very sad time for our people," Hawk replied with emotion.

"That's awful!" cried Jerome.

The boys sat in silence for a while, then Rico asked Hawk, "Are you supposed to say 'Native Americans' or 'Indians'?"

"Actually, both are acceptable," Hawk explained. "We were named Indians by an explorer who thought, when he reached America, that he had reached India. He was *really* confused. But the name has stuck. As long as you don't use the word in a negative way, and remember that we are the native people of this country, then 'Indian' is usually okay."

"I see," said Rashawn, "kinda like 'Black' and 'African American.'"

"Yes, a little," replied Hawk.

"Are you the chief of a big tribe?" asked Jerome.

"We have more than six hundred in our band here, but there are hundreds of thousands of Native people living all over this country, on reservations, in small towns, in big cities—everywhere. We are part of the American fabric just like you."

"Hey, Hawk-mon! Have you ever heard of Tecumseh?" asked Ziggy. "He was an Indian from Ohio. We learned about him in school."

"And what about Caesar?" added Rashawn. "We just found out that this park was named for a Black man who lived with the Shawnee. You know anything about him?"

"Tecumseh was not just 'an Indian from Ohio,'" Hawk replied with fire in his eyes. "He was the greatest Shawnee warrior ever to walk these lands, a hero to all generations.

"And yes, I know the story of Caesar as well. Tecumseh and Caesar were friends. Native Americans and African Americans shared much in years past. So much of that has been hidden by the shadows of time. Listen, and I will share with you the secrets and shadows of Caesar's Creek!"

Ten

"**Did Caesar have to do manhood ceremonies** like Tecumseh?" Rico wanted to know. "Our camp counselor told us about the winter challenge."

"Caesar might have had to prove his manhood when he was accepted into the tribe, but only boys had to do the winter ordeal," Hawk replied.

"She told us she was the great-great granddaughter of Caesar. Are you any relation to Tecumseh?" asked Jerome.

"No, son. But my spirit relates to him." Hawk paused for a moment. "Even as a child, Tecumseh was special. The night he was born, a great meteor streaked through the sky. It was a very special sign."

"You mean he didn't get cold when he jumped in that frozen water, mon?" Ziggy asked.

"Of course he was cold, but he had to learn to find the fire within himself and not feel the cold and the snow and the ice," Hawk explained.

"Wow! He was tougher than I could ever be," admitted Jerome. "I bet he ran back to his house when he got out of that frozen water!"

"Oh, no! Tecumseh walked back slowly and with dignity, as did his father before him," Hawk said with a proud smile.

"Were they glad to get to the last day of that ordeal?" asked Rashawn.

"Well, yes and no," Hawk replied. "On the last day of their three-month challenge, the boys had to jump into the frozen water four times. On the last jump, they had to go down to the bottom, and bring back whatever they put their hands on. Sometimes they would bring up grass, or dirt, or rocks; every once in a while, a boy would bring up something really special."

"What did Tecumseh find, mon?" Ziggy asked eagerly.

"It was a stone—but not just any stone. It glowed with different colors and changed as light shined on it. Sometimes it looked like the eye of a panther; sometimes like a star from the sky. It was very unusual and very special. And so was he."

"Awesome," whispered Rashawn.

"So how did Caesar know Tecumseh?" Jerome asked.

"Caesar came to the Shawnee when Tecumseh was about eight years old, probably right around the time of his winter manhood challenge. So Caesar would have been one of the elders who helped Tecumseh grow to be the great man he became."

The fire crackled, and Ziggy shivered as he glanced at the moon, which was fading as morning grew near. He remembered what Noni had said. *She was right, mon,* he thought. *A mystery moon,* she had whispered. *Strange events will happen tonight! Shadows walk in the moonlight.*

"It's almost morning," Rico said. Then, remembering the arrowhead he had found, he took it out of his pocket and gave it to Hawk. "We found this," he explained. "But I want you to have it. Maybe it belonged to Tecumseh or Caesar."

Hawk smiled as he glanced at the arrowhead. "This is very special, and I thank you for the gift. Perhaps it did once belong to one of the great ones. But I want you boys to keep it as my gift, as a memory of this night. Life must give to life," he said quietly.

"Thanks, Hawk," Rico said with feeling.

"Can you show us how to get back to our camp, Hawk?" Jerome asked. "This has been an amazing night, but we're gonna get killed if we don't get back!"

"Well, it looks like you boys got your night challenge anyway," Hawk said with a chuckle. "Let's head out of here, young braves!"

They were still a little damp, and really tired, but the four boys were ready to go. They followed Hawk, who knew the easy paths even in the darkness. The miles seemed to pass quickly as Hawk told them stories that his people had told to children for generations. Gradually the darkness faded and the shadows of the night were replaced by sunshine.

Ziggy's cheerful mood had returned with the daylight, and he laughed at the birds and squirrels as he jogged on the trail beside Hawk and the other boys.

"Look, mon!" he cried, as he picked up a bright red pebble, then an orange one, then a purple one. "They look like . . ."

"They're not pebbles!" cried Rico. "They're jelly beans! Brandy's jelly beans! We're almost there!"

Hawk grinned, proud that they were able to find the trail on their own. Soon the path widened, and the trees disappeared behind them. They stood once again on the edge of the huge meadow, which still shone with a golden glow. On the other side of the meadow lay the lake that had terrified them just a few hours before. To their left stood the two small tents and the remains of their fire. Noni and the girls ran toward them.

"Where have you *been*?" Noni yelled with relief

and anger. "We thought you were lost or hurt or worse!"

"We've been looking for you since before day-light!" Mimi reported.

"You're gonna get it!" warned Liza.

"Did you take that canoe out?" Tiana whispered to Rashawn. He nodded and smiled.

"It was fun at first. I'll tell you all about it later," he whispered back.

The boys introduced Hawk and tried to explain everything that had happened all at the same time. Once Noni understood that they were safe, she relaxed, but they knew they were still in big trouble.

Hawk said to her, "Don't be too hard on the young braves here. They did wrong, we know, but they passed their challenge like men. I'm very proud to know them."

Ziggy grinned with pride. "Thanks, mon. I have a gift for you, something I want you to have."

Rico, Rashawn, and Jerome shook Hawk's hand and thanked him once again. He hugged them and told them he had to go.

Hawk stooped down and gathered all eight children around him. "Come, my children," he said. "Remember the songs of the wind and the trees. Remember the secrets of the shadows. Life must give to life. *Tanakia*. Farewell."

"*Tanakia*, mon," said Ziggy softly. "'Bye."

Hawk turned to wave good-bye as he walked back into the woods. Noni and the children waved, calling their thanks to the tall, smiling Shawnee who proudly wore a slightly damp, many-pocketed, long purple coat.

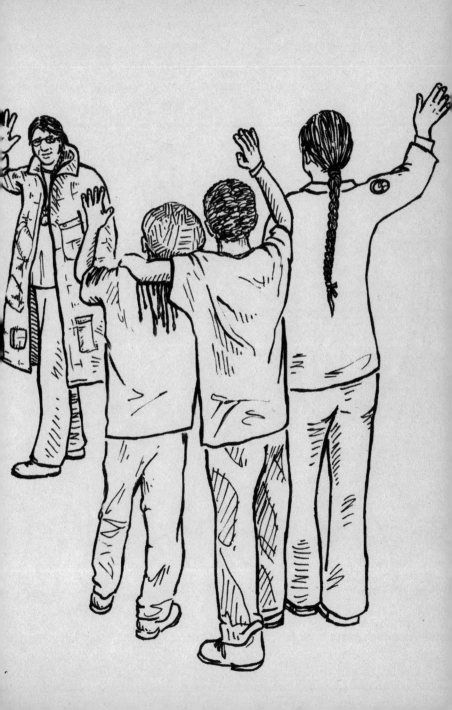

STUDY GUIDE FOR
Ziggy and the Black Dinosaurs #3:
Shadows of Caesar's Creek
by Sharon M. Draper

DISCUSSION TOPICS

CHAPTER 1

1-2. Ziggy is excited about the upcoming overnight camping trip. Write about one thing that might be fun about such a trip. Then write about one thing that might be a negative about such a trip.

3. Write or draw a description of Ziggy's backyard.

4. Write or draw a description of the clubhouse the boys built.

5. Write or draw a description of Ziggy. What does his description tell you about his personality?

6. Give several examples of Ziggy's unusual tastes in food.

7. If you were going on this camping trip, what

other items would you bring in addition to the things listed in chapter one? Why?

8-9. From the descriptions given in the first chapter, how are the four boys alike? How are they different?

10. Make a prediction: What is likely to happen on the camping trip?

CHAPTER 2

1-2. Describe how Jerome looks as the boys prepare to leave for the trip. What does he wear and what does he carry? What does that tell you about him?

3-4. Describe how Rico looks as they prepare to leave for the trip. What does he wear and what does he carry? What does that tell you about him?

5. Describe the girls who are on the trip.

6-7. Describe how Rashawn looks as the class prepares to leave for the trip. What do you think he decided to wear? What do you think he decided to carry with him? Why?

8-9. Describe how Ziggy looks as they prepare to leave for the trip. What does he wear and what does he carry? What does that tell you about him?

10. Who was Caesar and why does the park have his name?

CHAPTER 3

1. Who is Noni and what is her role on the trip?

2. Describe the pond.

3. What do the children notice at first?

4. What do they notice as they look closer?

5. What does Noni teach Ziggy about the capturing of animals?

6. Describe the woods the children walk through as they head for the campsite.

7. What is the difference between walking for a mile in the city and walking for a mile in the woods?

8. Who keeps eating and dropping jelly beans? Why do you think this is an important detail?

9. What does Ziggy learn about poison ivy?

10. What do the children learn about mayapples?

CHAPTER 4

1. How does Noni compare the way the children walk through the woods to the way Shawnee children walked?

2. Describe the process of putting up a tent and setting up a campsite.

3. If you were doing this, what difficulties might you encounter? What would you do about

rocks on the ground, or food, or water, or fire?

4. Describe Rashawn's lunch. What do you learn about his eating habits?

5. Describe Ziggy's lunch. What do you learn about his eating habits?

6. Describe or draw a picture of the scene after lunch.

7. What is the difference between what the boys are doing and what the girls are doing?

8. What do the boys find? Describe it.

9. Why do you think Ziggy whispers with respect?

10. Make a prediction: What is likely to happen because of finding the arrowhead?

CHAPTER 5

1. What is unusual about the arrowhead the boys find?

2. How does Rico tease Mimi? Is this realistic? Explain.

3. List several ways to make a fire in the woods. Which method does Noni use?

4. What is different about the meal the campers eat compared to the meals they would ordinarily eat at home?

5. Describe the canoe the boys find. What might it look like if it's old and has been there a long time?

6. Noni describes how the area looked three hundred years ago. What was different about the way it was then and the way it is today?

7. What images and memories do the children share about how Native Americans were treated in this country?

8. The children discuss how Africans were made slaves when they came to this country. Why

wasn't the enslavement of Native Americans a successful project?

9. How did Native Americans and runaway slaves work together?

10. How is Noni related to Caesar?

CHAPTER 6

1. Noni tells the children that the Revolutionary War was fought for freedom. Why do you think that freedom for slaves was not included?

2. Even though Caesar the slave is mentioned in a book of fiction, he was a real person who really lived in the Ohio valley. What job had he been trained for?

3. How did Caesar help the Shawnee Indians?

4. Why did the Shawnees give Caesar the land?

5. How long did Caesar live with the Shawnee Indians and what happened as a result?

6. What does Noni tell the children about chiefs and arrowheads?

7. How does Noni describe life in a Shawnee village?

8. What was the role of women in the village? What was the role of men in the village? Did women ever do what some might describe as a man's job?

9. Describe the Shawnee manhood ceremony that Ziggy demonstrates.

10. What other ceremonies does Noni tell them about?

CHAPTER 7

1. List several things that might make the night seem scary.

2. What makes you think the boys might be scared?

3. Why do the boys plan to sneak out of their tent?

4. What is their plan if they are discovered? Do they originally plan to use the canoe?

5. When they first get into the boat, they are just pretending. Who decides to put it into the water?

6. Why do they compare themselves to young Shawnee warriors?

7. How do you think the boys feel as they push the boat into the water?

8. What is Rico's attitude as they play with the boat? What does this tell you about him?

9. Where have they left the paddles?

10. How do you think the boys feel when they realize they are adrift?

CHAPTER 8

1. What makes the boat drift so far away so quickly?

2. Who else is aware of their plans to sneak out? Why is this a scary thought?

3. For what purpose do they use the FOR SALE sign? For what purpose do they use Ziggy's umbrella?

4. Make a prediction. How will the boys get rescued?

5. Paddling a boat seems to be a pretty easy task. What do the boys discover about moving a boat through water?

6. Why is it dangerous to stand up in a canoe?

7. How do you think it would feel to land in the water in the middle of the night?

8. What shows that Ziggy is scared? What is humorous about his fear?

9. What is different about the shore from which they left and the shore they land on?

10. Describe their walk through the woods at night. Why is this frightening as well as uncomfortable?

CHAPTER 9

1. What makes the boys run screaming in the darkness?

2. How do you know the boys are frightened? Do you think a bear is really chasing them?

3. Explain this statement: "Suddenly the tree moved!" Explain how the tree can talk.

4. Describe the man who rescues the boys.

5. Describe his dwelling and what he gives the boys.

6. Hawk wears glasses. Why do the boys think that is unusual for a Shawnee? What does that tell you about making assumptions?

7. What does Hawk tell them about the Shawnee people who lived in that area many years ago?

8. How does Hawk answer the question about whether "Native American" or "Indian" is the most acceptable term?

9. What does Hawk tell the boys about Native Americans living in this country today?

10. How does Hawk respond to the mention of Tecumseh?

CHAPTER 10

1. According to legend, what happened the night that Tecumseh was born?

2. According to legend, what did Tecumseh find on the final day of his manhood challenge? Why was it special?

3. How did Caesar assist in the upbringing of one of the greatest Shawnee warriors who ever lived?

4. How do Noni's predictions from chapter six about mysteries and strange events come true?

5. Why do you think Rico gives the arrowhead to Hawk?

6. Why do you think Hawk gives it back?

7. Explain this statement that Hawk makes: "Life must give to life."

8. What do the boys discover on the path that helps them find their way back?

9. Even though they may be in trouble for sneaking out, explain how what the boys did could be considered a successful night challenge.

10. What does Ziggy offer to Hawk as a gift? Why is this significant?

ADDITIONAL ACTIVITIES:

A. INFORMATION TO EXPLORE AND DISCOVER. Use the Internet, an encyclopedia, or books to find out more about the following:

1. Tecumseh, the warrior

2. *Tecumseh*, the outdoor drama

3. Shawnee Indians of three hundred years ago

4. Shawnee Indians today

5. Caesar Creek State Park

6. Arrowheads

7. Canoeing and camping

8. Hiking in the woods

9. Harness making

10. African Americans and Native Americans
   working together

B. JOBS TO EXPLORE:

1. Archaeologist

2. Camp director

3. Historian

4. Biographer

5. Naturalist

6. Forest ranger

7. Restoration expert

8. River guide

9. Environmental expert

10. Bird-watcher

C. WEB SITES TO EXPLORE:

www.caesarscreekvillage.org

www.dnr.state.oh.us/parks/parks/caesarck.htm

www.dnr.state.oh.us/dnap/location/caesar_creek.
  html

www.bluejacketdrama.com/tickets/buynow/

www.tecumsehdrama.com/frame_show.html?a=
shakespear&b=show&c=show

D. WRITING ACTIVITIES:

1. Using the Internet or newspaper ads from camping supply stores, find out what you'd need to go on a camping trip and how much it would cost. Write up a plan for your trip.

2. Find out what animals might be found roaming in the woods of an Ohio forest. Find out if it would be possible for Ziggy and his friends to be chased by a bear.

3. Write an essay about being afraid. You can write about what it is like for Ziggy and the boys, or you can write about a time when you were very frightened. Be sure to include the feelings and emotions that fear brings out.

4. Interview someone who is a Native American,

works with Native Americans, or knows something about all the Native Americans who are living in this country today. Write an essay about what you learn.

5. Write a poem or story about being brave.

6. Write a poem or story about adventures and challenges.

7. Write a newspaper story about how Ziggy and his friends get lost and then rescued in the park.

8. Find out about state parks in your state. Where are they located? What do they offer? You can go on the Internet to find this information. Many places will mail you brochures and maps.

9. Rashawn is afraid of insects. Research the insects in your area and find out which ones are dangerous and which ones are helpful. What would you tell Rashawn about what you've learned about bugs?

10. After you read and research about Tecumseh, write a poem or story about him.

11. "Can you imagine what it was like a long time ago when the Indians lived here?" Tiana spoke softly, looking at the quiet beauty around her. "It's so pretty!" Write a poem about the beauty of the world before civilization changed things.